DOCTOR
WHO

PUFFIN

BBC CHILDREN'S BOOKS

UK | USA | Canada | Ireland | Australia
India | New Zealand | South Africa

BBC Children's Books are published by Puffin Books,
part of the Penguin Random House group of companies
whose addresses can be found at global.penguinrandomhouse.com.

www.penguin.co.uk
www.puffin.co.uk
www.ladybird.co.uk

 Penguin
Random House
UK

First published 2020
001

Written by Chris Farnell

Illustrated by Dan Green

Printed and bound in Great Britain by Clays Ltd, Elcograf S.p.A.

A CIP catalogue record for this book is available from the British Library

ISBN: 978–1–405–94583–7

All correspondence to:
BBC Children's Books
Penguin Random House Children's
One Embassy Gardens, New Union Square
5 Nine Elms Lane, London SW8 5DA

BBC

DOCTOR WHO

KNOCK!
KNOCK!
WHO's
THERE?

JOKE BOOK

PUFFIN

CONTENTS

CONTENTS

THE FIRST DOCTOR

When is the Doctor late?

When he travels in his *TARDY-IS*.

Why does the TARDIS's tea-making machine only serve English Breakfast tea?

Because the *chamomile-ean* circuit is broken.

What did the Dalek say to the petrol pump?

'TAKE YOUR FINGER OUT OF YOUR EAR WHEN I AM EXTERMINATING YOU!'

The Doctor and his granddaughter, Susan, step out of the TARDIS.

'Where are we?' Susan asks.

'I don't know,' says the Doctor.

'When are we?' Susan asks.

'I don't know,' says the Doctor.

'Why's the sky that peculiar yellow colour?'

'I'm really not sure,' says the Doctor.

'What's that weird noise?' asks Susan.

The Doctor listens carefully, then says, **'I've got no idea.'**

'Grandfather,' Susan asks, 'does it annoy you when I ask lots of questions?'

The Doctor laughs and places a hand on Susan's shoulder. **'Of course not, my child! How else would you learn anything?'**

Which side of the TARDIS is biggest?

The inside!

What's the best place to get a sandwich on Skaro?

The *Dalek*-atessen.

What do you call it when Time Lords fight in the kitchen?

A *galley* fray.

SUSAN'S REJECTED LIST OF WHAT 'TARDIS' STANDS FOR

 This **A**lien **R**oadster **D**oes **I**t **S**tylishly

 Travels **A**t **R**andom **D**estinations **I**n **S**equence

 Tiny **A**rtefact **R**eally **D**isguises **I**nterior **S**ize

 Teleporting **A**imlessly **R**ound **D**elightful **I**ntergalactic **S**cenes

 Totally **A**wesome **R**adical **D**evastatingly **I**ncredible **S**paceship

 TARDIS **A**cronym **R**ecurs **D**ownwards **I**nfinite **S**teps

 Time **A**nd **R**elative **D**imension **I**n **S**pace

THE SECOND DOCTOR

'I've just found a planet with a big tomb full of Cybermen!'

'Telos?'

'I'm telling everyone!'

Jamie: This moon base is incredible, Doctor. I can jump higher than a lamp post!

Doctor: I should think so, Jamie. You see, lamp posts can't jump.

What's the Macra's favourite card game?

Snap!

Did you hear what happened to all the rockets when they invented the transmat?

They got fired.

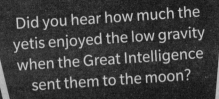

Did you hear how much the yetis enjoyed the low gravity when the Great Intelligence sent them to the moon?

They were woolly jumpers.

What do you sing on an Ice Warrior's birthday?

'Freeze a jolly good fellow!'

What do Ice Warriors put on their toast?

Mars-malade.

'YOU'VE REDECORATED, I DON'T LIKE IT.'

REJECTED TARDIS DESKTOP THEMES

INFLATABLE

Whenever the Vinvocci came round, their spikes kept bursting things.

UNDERWATER

Spills whenever you open the TARDIS doors.

M.C. ESCHER

People kept getting lost on the staircase.

STRAW/TWIGS

These themes tended to fall apart whenever the Doctor encountered the 'Bad Wolf' phenomenon. Bricks were okay though.

SMALLER ON THE INSIDE

Too cramped.

PEARS

The taste proved unpopular.

THE THIRD DOCTOR

... **timing!**

The secret of Gallifreyan comedy is ...

Do those living shop-window dummies ever need their batteries changed?

No. They Auton, and on, and on, and on.

TOP SECRET

Where do UNIT keep their armies?

Up their sleevies.

Brigadier: Doctor, where are you?

Doctor: I'm just taking Bessie for a spin along the M4.

Brigadier: Careful out there, Doctor. Apparently, there's a madman driving up the motorway the wrong way!

Doctor: A madman? Brigadier, there are hundreds of them!

How do Silurians weigh themselves?

On the scales.

Why hasn't the Doctor defeated the Chronovore yet?

It's very time-consuming.

UNIT are investigating reports of a spaceship shaped like two rashers of bacon, a Cumberland sausage and an egg. They are asking for witnesses to come forward with any information about the **U**nidentified **F**rying **O**bject.

The Silurians have fantastic gardens in their underground cities. It's because they've all got **green fingers**.

The Master once told his arch nemesis, 'We're not so different, you and I.'

The Doctor was outraged. 'Don't be ridiculous: you're an evil megalomaniac, while I try to help people. Name one thing we have in common.'

The Master answered, **'Well, for starters, we have the same first name.'**

Why won't the Sea Devils dare fight shellfish?

Because of their big _mussels_.

'The invisible humanoids of Spiridon are great warriors, but terrible liars.'

'Why's that?'

'You can see right through them.'

THE MASTER IS IN!

PART ONE

'Master! Master! Will your tissue compression eliminator really cure me?'

'You just need to be a little patient.'

'Master! Master! I've only got 59 seconds to live!'

'Just wait a minute.'

'Master! Master! Is it true exercise kills germs?'

'Probably, but how do you get germs to exercise?'

'Master! Master! I think somebody wiped my memory.'

'When did that happen?'

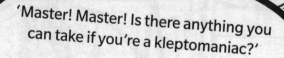

'Master! Master! Is there anything you can take if you're a kleptomaniac?'

'Whatever you like, I imagine.'

THE FOURTH DOCTOR

Where do Sontarans clean their uniforms?

At the dry clone-rs.

What did the Fourth Doctor's scarf say to his hat?

'I'll go around, and you go on ahead.'

What's K-9 short for?

He's not got any legs.

When K-9's feeling healthy he speaks very well for a dog, but when he catches a computer virus he sounds a bit *ruff*.

Doctor: My dog's got no nose.

Romana: Really? How does he smell?

K-9: A complex array of olfactory sensor devices, Mistress.

One day Romana walked into the TARDIS kitchen to see the Doctor staring grimly at his alphabetti spaghetti.

'What's wrong?' she asked.

'This,' the Doctor said, pointing to his bowl, **'spells disaster.'**

What's the best way to photograph a Mandrel?

From a very long way away!

Why have Krynoids started growing apples?

Because they heard one a day keeps the Doctor away.

'K-9! While you were making a copy of your hard drive, you reversed over my foot!'

'Apologies, Master. I was backing myself up.'

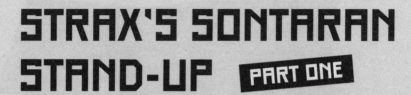

STRAX'S SONTARAN STAND-UP

PART ONE

A Sontaran walks into a bar.

There are no survivors.

BAR

Why did the Sontaran cross the road?

Because the other side of the road must be conquered!

A patient came to me and said, 'Strax! I feel like a pair of curtains!'

I told him, **'That will not matter when your world is crushed by the might of the Sontaran empire.'**

What do you say to a man with a wooden head?

Die, wooden-headed human scum!

What do you call a man with a spade in his head?

Merely the first casualty in the Sontarans' glorious subjugation of this garden centre!

You know, people often say to me, **'Please! Stop! We surrender!'**

THE FIFTH DOCTOR

Does the Doctor pick his nose?

No – with regeneration you never know what you're going to get.

Why does the Fifth Doctor wear a stick of celery?

Well, you don't want a leek on a spaceship, do you?

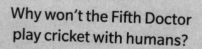

What's a Cyberman's favourite tea?

Fission chips.

Why won't the Fifth Doctor play cricket with humans?

He thinks it's kinder to use a bat and ball.

'Cyborg pirates have started stealing body parts and then selling them back to their owners.'

'Oh no! How much do the pirates make them pay?'

'A buck-an-ear.'

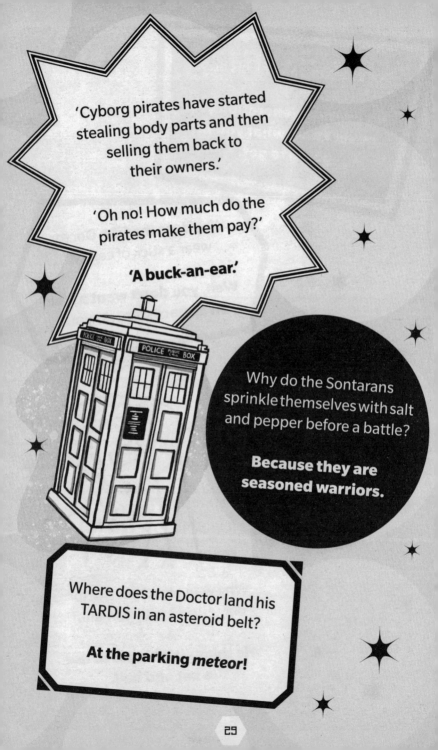

Why do the Sontarans sprinkle themselves with salt and pepper before a battle?

Because they are seasoned warriors.

Where does the Doctor land his TARDIS in an asteroid belt?

At the parking *meteor*!

DALEK BOOK CLUB

Eggs, Stir, Minute: Quick Recipes You Can Cook with Only an Egg Whisk and a Sink Plunger

War and Also Some More War

Daleks are from Skaro, Cybermen are from Mondas

The Very Angry Caterpillar

To Kill a Mockingbird (and Everyone Else)

The Dalek Emperor's New Clothes

Eat, Prey, Exterminate

I'm OK, You're Dead

THE SIXTH DOCTOR

Why shouldn't the Doctor meet himself?

It could cause a *pair-o'-docs*.

Why did the Cybermen stop at the service station?

For a quick *byte*.

Which outer-space monster can the Doctor most easily outrun?

Snail-liens.

How do you organise a surprise party for the Doctor?

You *plan-et*.

Who's the best chef on Gallifrey?

The *Thyme* Lord.

Where does the Doctor go to the toilet?

His *TURD-IS*.

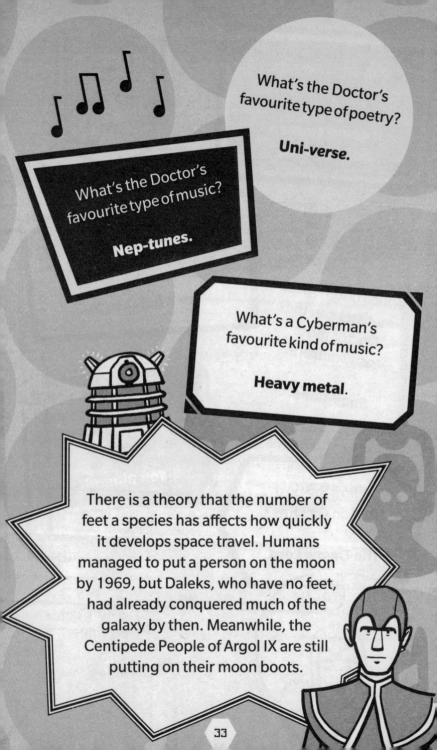

What's the Doctor's favourite type of poetry?

Uni-verse.

What's the Doctor's favourite type of music?

Nep-tunes.

What's a Cyberman's favourite kind of music?

Heavy metal.

There is a theory that the number of feet a species has affects how quickly it develops space travel. Humans managed to put a person on the moon by 1969, but Daleks, who have no feet, had already conquered much of the galaxy by then. Meanwhile, the Centipede People of Argol IX are still putting on their moon boots.

THE SEVENTH DOCTOR

Why was the Sixth Doctor scared of the Seventh Doctor?

Because seven ate nine.

Why doesn't the Seventh Doctor lose at cards?

Because he always has an Ace up his sleeve.

One day, the Doctor and the Master were walking across a jungle planet, when they heard the mighty roar of a Drashig.

Immediately the Master knelt down and swapped his shoes for a pair of trainers.

'What are you doing?' asked the Doctor.

'Getting ready to run!' the Master said. 'That Drashig's going to eat the first thing it finds.'

'Don't be an idiot!' the Doctor shouted. 'Drashigs are some of the greatest hunters in the universe. You can't just outrun them!'

'I don't need to outrun them,' the Master said, tying his laces and standing up.
'I just need to outrun you.'

The first time Fenric played the Doctor at chess he lost because he moved the castle first.

It was a rook-ie error.

On the TARDIS controls, what key does the Doctor press to visit other planets?

The space bar.

Did you hear the Master blasted the Doctor with a ray that turned him into a giant calendar?

His days are numbered.

The Doctor's reading a fascinating book about zero gravity.

He can't put it down. (Although, of course, the Doctor usually prefers to read **comet**-books.)

'Knock! Knock!'

'Who's there?'

'Interrupting Dalek.'

'Interrupting Dalek wh–'

'EXTERMINATE!'

THE MASTER IS IN!

PART TWO

'Master! Master! Did you just cut off the entire left side of that person's body?'

'Yes, but he's all right now.'

'Master! Master! I snore so much it's keeping me awake!'

'Sleep in the other room, then!'

'Master! Master! People keep ignoring me!'

'Next!'

'Master! Master! I'm turning into a pack of cards!'

'I'll deal with you later.'

'Master! Master! Why have you trapped me in a washing machine?'

'There's something going round.'

THE EIGHTH DOCTOR

The TARDIS is stranded because the chameleon circuit turned it the wrong colour.

It's marooned.

What do Daleks do when life gives them lemons?

Make extermin-ade.

How do Cybermen clean their feet before coming into the spaceship?

They wipe them on the Cybermat.

What's green and invisible?

No aliens.

POLICE PUBLIC CALL BOX

The Sisterhood of Karn believe they've discovered the secret to immortality.

But it will take forever to test.

FROM THE LINDA DATABASE

THE SECRET INCARNATIONS OF THE DOCTOR

Here at the London Investigations 'N' Detective Agency (LINDA) we have worked hard to keep tabs on all of the Doctor's faces throughout the years. We heard that he (or she) only had 13 lives, so naturally we were well pleased when we realised we had all thirteen faces. But then Mr Skinner tells us that he got a bunch of second-hand files from a UNIT car boot sale and apparently there's a secret 'War' Doctor as well.

So we thought, okay, fourteen Doctors. Maybe they, like, found an extra life or something. But then Bridget says she heard a rumour about this woman called Ruth in Gloucester and she was the Doctor as well. Then Bliss told us about this guy at the National Gallery, but he's a "Curator" not a Doctor, so that doesn't count.

But anyway, it looks like there's a lot more Doctors than we thought there were, so here's a list of some of the more embarrassing ones we've heard rumours about.

Elton Pope

THE WAR DOCTOR

The time-weapons used in the Last Great Time War often caused time jumps that meant the Gallifreyan soldiers skipped their mealtimes.

So they went back four seconds.

'Did you hear that Gallifrey genetically engineered some fearsome beasts to protect time from the Daleks?'

'No.'

'They called them watch dogs.'

What's worse than meeting your regenerated future-self?

If you're both wearing the same outfit.

'Did it take the War Doctor long to wipe out the Daleks and the Time Lords?'

'Just a Moment!'

UNIT AUTOPSY REPORT

TOP SECRET

The following are extracts from the autopsy of the strange alien life-form that was found in the wreck of a spaceship that crashed into Big Ben. After he handed in his report the medical examiner in charge was punished severely, although he swears every word of the report is true and he didn't tell any porkies.

The alien life-form appears to mostly resemble the Earth species *Sus scrofa domesticus*, or the common domestic pig. While I don't know how my colleagues transported the body to my lab from the crash site, I expect they used a hambulance.

During the crash the alien pilot appeared to suffer slight burns, which might have been treated with a special oinkment.

Despite the best efforts of paramedics at the scene, it appears they were unable to save its bacon.

Even if we had been able to keep the creature alive, its spaceship appears to be ruined beyond repair, making it a ground hog.

In conclusion, it seems pigs *can* fly, but not very well.

THE NINTH DOCTOR

Did you hear about when the Ninth Doctor became a vampire?

He was *fang-tastic!*

Did you hear about the actor from the Forest of Cheem?

Her performance was very wooden.

Why couldn't the Gelth go into the pub?

They don't serve spirits.

48

At what time did Blon Fel-Fotch Passameer-Day Slitheen devour the British Prime Minister?

At ate P.M.

Rose: Doctor, what's a light year?

Doctor: Like a normal year, but with fewer calories.

Why couldn't the Face of Boe go to the ball?

He had no *body* to go with.

How do nanobots say hello?

Microwaves.

Why are Daleks
bad at dancing?

**They can't
handle the steps.**

What happened to
the Weeping Angel
that saw its reflection?

It was petrified.

SATELLITE 5 GAMESHOWS

MY HAZMAT SUIT HAS A RIP IN IT, GET ME OUT OF HERE!

Slapstick fun ahoy as celebrities are sent into quarantined plague ships with safety equipment provided by the lowest bidder!

THE GREAT BRITISH TAKE OFF

Enthusiastic members of the public are given an hour to build a fully functioning liquid-propellant launch rocket, with hilarious (and sometimes fatal) results.

JUST A MINUTE

Members of the public compete to reach the end of our famous orbital obstacle course without hesitation, deviation or repetition, all before their limited oxygen supply runs out!

HOMES UNDER THE HAMMER

Our presenter helps families find a new place to live and move all their things in before their old house is attacked by a giant robot with a mallet.

THROUGH THE KEYHOLE

Contestants are locked in a room with a starving Slatherine beast from the Rabidon sector, with only one way out.

BARGAIN HUNT

Celebrity Bounty Hunters track down contestants for sport with only a low budget range of weaponry and tracking equipment.

STRICTLY COMET DANCING

High-speed, low-temperature dancing competition, where contestants wear spangly outfits that really aren't suitable for the vacuum of space.

ONLY CONNECT

Members of the public are locked in a gutted spaceship that contains only the wires and adaptors we found in that bottom drawer in the back room. The players must figure out which wires connect where to get the ship functional before it falls into the sun.

HAVE I GOT KILLER ROBOTS FOR YOU?

Self-explanatory dash for survival.

THE TENTH DOCTOR

Is that short alien with the big skull helmet feeling okay?

No, he's a little Sick-orax.

What's the Tenth Doctor's favourite letter?

A long C!

What is a Catkind's favourite breakfast cereal?

Mice crispies.

The Krillitane infiltrated a circus. They ate the ringmaster, they ate the lion tamer, and they ate all the acrobats, but they didn't eat the clowns because they tasted funny.

Did you hear Madame de Pompadour tell the court she was attacked by some clockwork robots?

I think she's winding them up.

Did you hear the Abzorbaloff is on a seafood diet?

He sees food, he eats it.

How do the Racnoss communicate?

The World Wide Web

'I was just photographing my friend when he turned into a big pile of fat babies . . .'

'Adipose?'

'No, it was more of a candid shot.'

Did you hear about when the head of Ood Operations was turned into an Ood himself?

Hair today, gone tomorrow!

'I've just been stung by a Vespiform!'

'Well, put some cream on it.'

'But it's already flown away!'

What do Carrionites eat in the desert?

Sand-wiches.

What do you call a spacesuit with a skeleton inside shoutin' Who turned out the lights? while flying a spaceship?

Crashed-a Narada.

People think the Ice Warriors ruled Mars, but actually the Flood **rained** there for years.

57

'Knock! Knock!'

'Who's there?'

'Doctor!'

'Doctor, **when?**'

'Well, remember when we followed a Silurian, a Judoon and a Hath into a bar and they all started arguing over how to change a light bulb? I think it started then.'

JUDOON POLICE REPORTS

Apprehended the fugitive known as 'the Master'. The Master escaped by giving the arresting officer a card with 'Please turn over' written on both sides.

Report #5493
A Judoon trooper pulled over a blue time vehicle with 'Police Box' written over the door. The Judoon knocked on the door, and was alarmed to discover the vehicle's passengers included a driver going by the name 'the Doctor', and a wild Betelgeusian Tiger.

TRANSCRIPT
Judoon: Why do you have a Betelgeusian Tiger in your vehicle
'Doctor': He's my friend.
Judoon: 'It is against the law to keep a Betelgeusian Tiger in your vehicle. Take him to the zoo.
'Doctor': Of course, officer, I'm sorry. I'll take him straight away.

Report #5494

The outlaw known as 'The Master' was sighted outside a supermarket. Judoon troopers chased him through the shop, but he evaded capture. The troopers were later found in the drinks aisle staring very hard at a carton of orange juice concentrate.

Report #5495

A squadron of Judoon troopers spent all night trying to find out why the sun had disappeared. Then it dawned on them.

Report #5496

A gang of intergalactic jewel thieves has been robbing planets in alphabetical order.

We suspect it's organised crime.

Report #5497

A Judoon trooper pulled over a blue time vehicle a second time. 'The Doctor' still had an illegal Betelgeusian Tiger on board.

TRANSCRIPT

Judoon: You were ordered to take this tiger to the zoo.
'Doctor': I did! He loved it.
Now we're going to the fairground.

Report #5498

Judoon troopers thought they had 'the Master' cornered in a launderette, but he made a clean getaway.

Report #5499

Judoon detectives have investigated a spate of toilet thefts throughout this sector. So far they have nothing to go on.

Report #5500

Judoon troopers have brought in some robots that had gone on a rampage downtown. They were arrested for assault and battery.

Report #5501

A squadron of Judoon was seen leaving the station with blankets over their heads today. Apparently they had been ordered to work undercover.

Report #5502

Today two Judoon troopers brought in a robber who tried to rob the Bank of Karabraxos. She would have got away with it, if she hadn't accidentally fallen into a vat of wet cement during her escape. The arresting officer said she was a hardened criminal.

Judoon troopers purchased a special set of active camouflage Judoon armour, but now we can't find it.

THE ELEVENTH DOCTOR

What's yellow and orange
and dangerous?

**Shark-infested
fish fingers and custard.**

What do you call an Atraxi
with three eyes?

Atrax-iii.

How can you tell if you have a star
whale under your bed?

Your nose touches the ceiling.

How does the sentient
planet of Akhaten keep its
trousers up?

With an asteroid belt.

How does Akhaten get clean?

Meteor showers.

Why are Vortex Manipulators built on to wristbands?

Because if they were built on to belts it would be a *waist* of time.

Why didn't Rory and Amy enjoy going on honeymoon?

It was too sticky.

What about when Rory and Amy went to a restaurant on the moon?

They found it had no atmosphere.

One day, the Eleventh Doctor was showing Amy and Rory around the TARDIS when they came to a room with a huge helter-skelter.

'What's this?' asked Rory.

'Oh this is my anything slide,' said the Doctor. 'It's quite clever – as you go down the slide, you shout out what you want, and the telepathic circuits will tune into what you say and materialise a big heap of it at the bottom.'

'That's ridiculous,' said Rory.

'Is it? Watch this!' said the Doctor, and leaped on to the helter-skelter, shouting, 'JELLY BABIES!'

Rory and Amy looked over the side of the slide and, sure enough, the Doctor was sitting at the bottom in a big pile of jelly babies.

'That looks fun. I want a go,' Amy said, and before Rory could stop her she'd climbed on to the slide and was speeding down it, shouting, 'CHOCOLATE!'

Rory looked over the side and saw Amy sitting happily in a huge mountain of chocolate.

'Maybe it's not so bad after all,' Rory said, climbing on to the slide and setting off.

The Doctor was right, the slide was so much fun. So much fun, in fact, that Rory cried out **'Wheeeeeee!'** all the way down . . .

Did you hear that the Silence decided to put on a play?

To be honest, it was pretty forgettable.

Knock! Knock!

Who's there?

The Silence.

The Silence who?

Knock! Knock!

Who's there?

The Silence.

The Silence who?

Knock! Knock!

Who's there?

Madame Kovarian: We've done it! We've kidnapped Melody Pond!

Kovarian's Trusted Lieutenant: Well done, Ma'am. But how can we get a baby to sleep on a spaceship?

Madame Kovarian: You rock-et.

How many Weeping Angels does it take to change a lightbulb?

Three. One to hold the ladder, one to change the bulb, and one to turn the light off afterwards so they can move again.

How many tickets did the Cybermen buy to get into Hedgewick's World of Wonders?

None – they got in free of charge.

How can you find out how many aliens died in the skies above Trenzalore?

Check the *orbit*-uaries.

Which dinosaur do Weeping Angels fear most?

Doyouthinkhesaurus.

THE LAST QUESTION

It used to be a well-known fact that the Doctor only had thirteen lives. However, a number of recent developments have cast that in doubt; firstly when the Time Lords gave her more regenerations at Trenzalore, and then with the revelation that she may have had more incarnations in the past.

What this means is that hypothetically, if the light on the top of the TARDIS malfunctioned, and the Doctor electrocuted herself trying to fix it, there's no telling how many times she might regenerate before the power went out.

So, ultimately, the question is: how many Doctors can a lightbulb change?

STRAX'S SONTARAN STAND-UP PART TWO

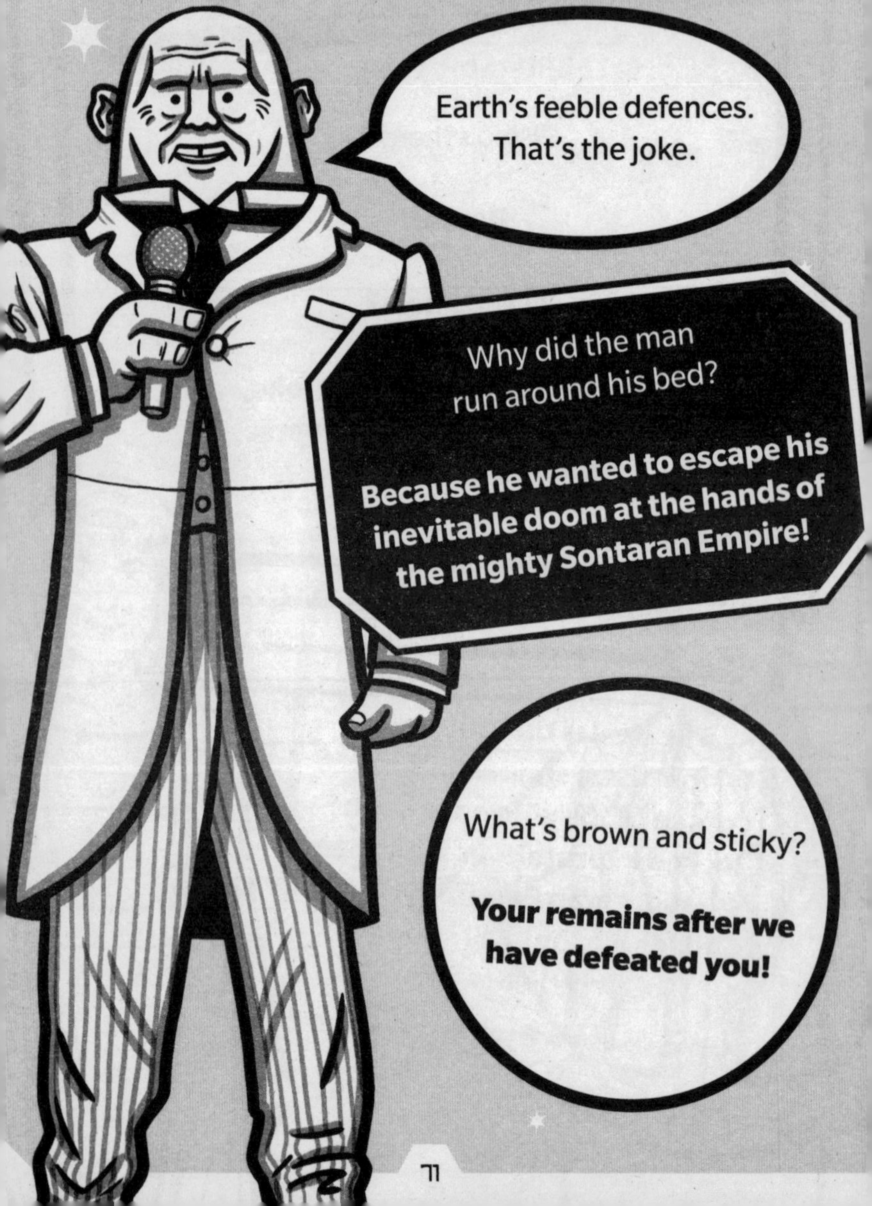

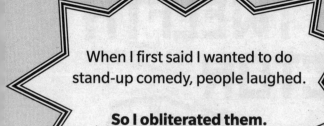

When I first said I wanted to do stand-up comedy, people laughed.

So I obliterated them.

What's worse than finding a maggot in an apple?

The Fifth Sontaran Death Fleet!

What is the deal with 'Rutans'?

The deal is that they are formless, shapeshifting green blobs who have been locked in brutal war with the Sontaran Empire for millennia, but will soon be utterly destroyed.

THE TWELFTH DOCTOR

Once the Twelfth Doctor was locked up in a dungeon with Robin Hood.

They both managed to get out, but it was an *arrow* escape.

How do you make a Zygon laugh?

With ten-*tickles*!

I'm not saying you're stupid, but if the Teller of the Bank of Karabraxos ate your brain, he'd still have room for dessert.

The Doctor has fought Cybermen, Judoon and Plasmavores on Earth's moon, but the craziest enemy he faced there has to be that species of giant parasitic insects.

They were *luna-ticks*.

Do you think the people of Earth are still upset about that time their nearest satellite turned out to be an egg that was hatching?

No, they're over the moon.

Why won't the Mummy on the Orient Express listen to anyone?

He's too wrapped up in himself.

What do the Kantrofarri dream crabs like to watch on their night off?

Cling films.

Professor River Song is a galaxy-famous archaeologist. So why doesn't she have very good career prospects?

Because her job's in ruins.

How does River Song find hieroglyphs?

They're above the lower-oglyphs.

I thought the Shoal of the Winter Harmony were plotting to take over the Earth by replacing all our brains, but they changed my mind.

What do you call the frozen space travellers aboard the colony ship Erehwon?

Ice-tronauts.

Do you ever wonder what would happen if an elephant saw the Silence?

Why did the Emojibots demand a holiday?

So they could recharge their batteries.

THE MASTER IS IN!

PART THREE

'Master! Master! I've broken my arm in two places!'

'Don't go back there then!'

'Master! Master! You didn't have to stick that massive needle in my hand!'

'You have a point.'

'Master! Master! Wherever I stand, I seem to drill a hole into the ground!'

'You're boring.'

'Master! Master! I can't sleep now you've suspended my hospital bed over an active volcano!'

'Don't worry, you'll soon drop off.'

'Master! Master! There's something awful on my neck!'

'Yes, it's your head.'

THE THIRTEENTH DOCTOR

Why couldn't the Doctor sneak past the mutant arachnids?

They *spied* 'er.

How do you know if a Pting has got into your fridge?

There are footprints in the butter.

Why is Earth the Doctor's favourite planet?

All it has to do is turn around once and it makes her day.

How does the Doctor pay for coffee in space?

With Star Bucks.

Why couldn't the Kerb!am Man get his deliveries to the right address?

He had a screw loose.

Yaz: My dad just bought one of those universal remote controls.

Doctor: **But that changes everything!**

Dorium Maldovar, the Moxx of Balhoon, Chantho and Tzim-Sha have started a support group.

It's for people who are feeling blue.

Once the Doctor heard a rumour about a starship made of spaghetti. Did she believe it?

Not at first, but then it flew straight *pasta*.

'Oh no, a Pting is going to eat the Earth!'

'What's that then?'

'It's a big planet with people on it, but that's not important right now.'

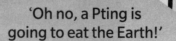

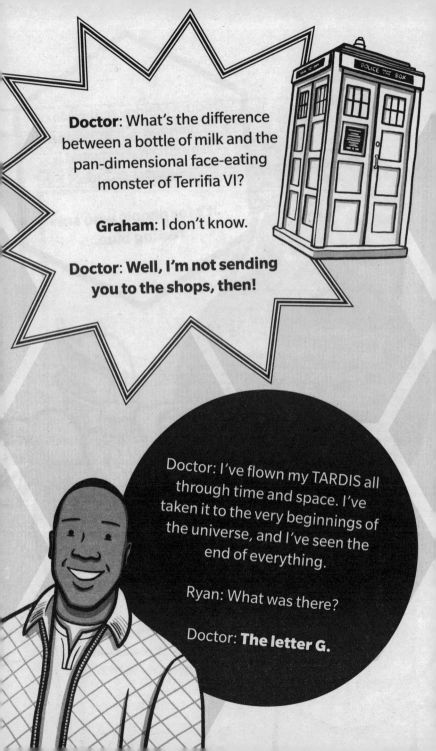

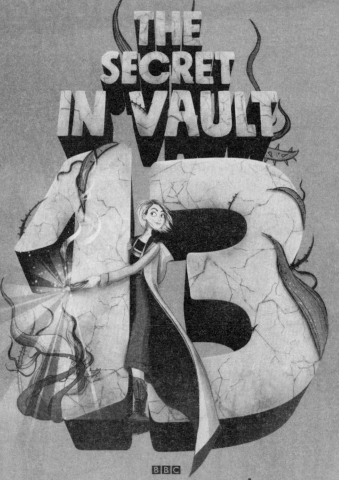

PILL 14-01-21.